DATE DUE

DISCARD

DISNEY · PIXAR
FINDING DORY

Hank the Septopus

A
Disarming
Tale

By
Amy Sky Koster

Illustrated by the
Disney Storybook Art Team

A Random House PICTUREBACK® Book

Random House 🏠 New York

Copyright © 2016 Disney Enterprises, Inc., and Pixar. All rights reserved. Published in the United States by Random House Children's Books,
a division of Penguin Random House LLC, 1745 Broadway, New York, NY 10019, and in Canada by Penguin Random House Canada Limited, Toronto, in conjunction
with Disney Enterprises, Inc. Pictureback, Random House, and the Random House colophon are registered trademarks of Penguin Random House LLC.

randomhousekids.com

ISBN 978-0-7364-3510-9

Printed in the United States of America

10 9 8 7 6 5 4 3 2 1

E
CC 2290
$ 13.49
2/17

Hank, I just realized something. An **octopus** has eight arms, but you only have seven—that makes you a **septopus**!

Hank?
Where'd you go?

There you are!
You were going to tell me
about your lost **farm**—
I mean, **arm**!

All right, I give up.
Here's the story. . . .

WHAT? C'mon.
That didn't happen.

Okay, okay.
You got me.

It was actually a **trapeze** accident.

Sorry, that was a fib. Truth is, I was a
dog walker—but **not** for long!

That's **amazing**!

But there was also that time
I was a **cowboy** . . .

. . . and a **ninja**, too.

Just kidding. I'm pulling your **fin**.
I lost my arm while I was
in a **rock band**.

Or maybe it happened
during an
**arm-wrestling
match.**

I wish **I** had arms. . . . **Hey, Hank!** I just **remembered**—you lost *your* arm! How did you become a **septopus**?

Well, Dory— it all started when I went **back in time** to save the world. . . .